ALIEN HARVEST

BY MELANIE JOYCE

ILLUSTRATED BY ALEKSANDER SOTIROVSKI

Titles in Ignite II

Alien Harvest	Melanie Joyce
Blackbeard's Treasure	Roger Hurn
Chocolate Wars	Andy Seed
The Hamster Who Fell to Earth	Danny Pearson
Jimmy, Donkey of the Somme	Clare Lawrence
Night Wolf	Jonny Zucker
The Princess and the Knight	Helen Orme
Silent Screen	Mike Gould
Snow Beast	Craig Allen
Zombie Goldfish	Danny Pearson

Badger Publishing Limited
Oldmedow Road,
Hardwick Industrial Estate,
King's Lynn PE30 4JJ
Telephone: 01438 791037

www.badgerlearning.co.uk

2 4 6 8 10 9 7 5 3

Alien Harvest ISBN 978-1-78147-456-3

Publisher: Susan Ross
Senior Editor: Danny Pearson
Publishing Assistant: Jennifer Brough
Design: Fiona Grant
Illustration: Aleksander Sotirovski
Copyeditor: Ursula Faulkner

ALIEN HARVEST

Contents

Vocabulary:

dribbled   examine

identical   jerked

landed   planet

routine   scanned

voyage   wriggled

Main characters:

Galen

Neshla

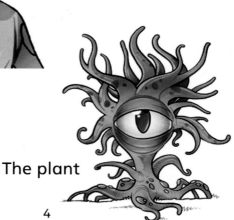

The plant

Chapter 1

Voyage

Earth, 5014

Galen's father read the mail message out loud. "Routine virus scan. Vetron 5."

"If it's a routine scan, can Neshla come too?" asked Galen.

Dad was head of the Food Unit that supplied Earth. He had to check the food planets for viruses.

It was just routine. What harm could it do?

At the space hub, the transport ship was ready.

"Ready?" asked Dad.

"Ready," replied Galen and his best friend, Neshla.

The ship lifted from the hub dock. It shot into space.

"Vetron 5 is low risk for alien life," said Dad, "but be careful."

"We'll be careful!" said Galen and Neshla.

Hours passed.

Finally, the ship landed. "Welcome to Vetron 5," said Dad.

He set off to start the scan.

Galen and Neshla looked around.
The planet had two moons.

Its surface was covered with growth pods.

"Find me if you can!" said Neshla.
She ducked into a huge pod.

It was full of small plants.

"I'll find you!" called Galen. He looked for ages.

Then, Galen saw something. Was that
an eye staring at him?

"Got you, Neshla!" he cried.

It wasn't Neshla. It was a plant.
The flower was identical to a human
eye.

"That's weird," said Galen. He reached
out to touch the plant.

"Ouch!" said Galen. A trickle of blood ran down his finger. He suddenly felt dizzy.

Neshla was calling. "It's time to go," she said.

The eye moved. "Yes," said Galen.

He pulled out the plant. He put it into his pocket.

It was time to board the ship.

Chapter 2

Secrets

Dad put the ship on autopilot.

"How about some dinner?" he said.

Galen was quiet.

"You look strange," said Neshla.

"No, I don't," snapped Galen. He sprang up from the table.

"I'm going to my room."

Galen grabbed a heavy bag of something. He stormed off.

Galen had never snapped at Neshla before. What was the matter with him?

Neshla followed Galen to his room. She was about to knock when she heard voices.

Galen was speaking to someone. Who was he talking to?

Neshla knocked on the door.

The door opened slightly.

An eye stared at Neshla. It looked scared.

"Who are you talking to?" asked Neshla.

"No one," snapped Galen. "Go away."

He slammed the door. There was something wrong. Galen had changed. It was since he had been on Vetron 5.

What had happened there?

Neshla ran to tell his dad.

Galen's dad listened to Neshla.

"There's something else," he said. "Most of the fresh meat has gone."

Dad and Neshla ran to Galen's room. Dad banged on the door.

The door creaked open. Galen looked different. His eyes were glassy and blank. Behind him, something was moving.

Chapter 3

The host

The plant was on Galen's desk. It had grown to the size of an adult dog.

In its centre was a large eye.

"What's that doing on board?" snapped Dad. "It could be dangerous."

Galen backed towards the plant.

"Not dangerous," he said. "Hungry."

Neshla stared at her friend. "Galen, why have you been taking meat from the cold store?"

Galen stared at her. He stared at the plant. Then he laughed.

"This isn't a joke," said Dad, angrily.

He pushed past Galen. He jerked the plant up by the roots.

"This is going into the isolation lab," said Dad. "I'll talk to you later, Galen."

Dad stormed off.

Neshla turned to Galen. "Why did you bring that on board?" she asked.

"The eye told me to," said Galen.

The doors of the isolation lab swished open. Dad needed to examine the plant.

"Let's examine you and see what you are," he said.

Suddenly, the mail dock bleeped. There was a new message.

"They want the virus report," said Dad.

He looked at the plant. "You'll have to wait," he said.

Neshla picked up a leaf. It had fallen from the plant. She went to her room.

Neshla scanned the leaf across her computer screen. Data began to appear.

Neshla read it.

```
Species: Eltrapod
Origin: Vargon/Alien
Alert: Meat-eating.
Aggressive. Cannot
tolerate water.
DANGER.
```

They were all in danger.

Chapter 4

Red alert

Neshla raced to Galen's room.

"Your dad's in danger," she shouted. "Come on, hurry!"

Neshla dragged Galen along like a rag doll.

Suddenly, there was a terrible scream.

Neshla opened the lab door. The plant had grown bigger.

It had grabbed Galen's dad.

The eye waved about madly.

Thorny tentacles wriggled like snakes.

Underneath, a drooling mouth gaped.
It was lined with rows of razor-sharp teeth.

"Help me," gasped Dad. He could hardly
breathe.

Neshla needed to do something. What could she do?

The thing was growing before her eyes.

The creature gnashed its teeth.

Saliva dribbled down the quivering leaves.

"Hurry, it's preparing to feed," said Dad.

Neshla had to think quickly.

The creature wanted meat. Neshla ran to the meat store.

She grabbed a dish of raw meat.

The blood splashed onto her clothes.
Neshla ran to the lab.

The smell of blood made the creature
stop. It released Galen's dad.

Tentacles shot out and grabbed the
meat.

There was a squelching sound. Then it
stopped. The giant eye looked at Neshla.

It smelled the blood on her clothes.
"Get it into the airlock!" shouted Dad.

The creature shuffled towards Neshla.
She backed, step by step, towards the
airlock.

What if she got sucked into space with
the creature? What if she was its next
meal?

"I've got to try," thought Neshla.
"Otherwise, we'll all die."

Chapter 5

Deep space

Neshla was at the airlock. She could smell the creature.

It was getting closer. The head stretched towards her.

Saliva dribbled onto her head. Tentacles wrapped around her. They squeezed and squeezed.

She was going to die. Then, Neshla remembered about the water.

"Get water," she croaked.

The creature moved closer.

The eye swayed over Neshla. She could see the veins pulsing.

It was going to strike.

Dad grabbed the fire hose. Suddenly, there was a loud SWOOSH.

Water gushed into the airlock.

There was a hissing, screeching sound. The monster screamed. It twisted and groaned. Its eye turned red with anger.

Tentacles bashed against the airlock walls. They dented the thick metal.

"Neshla, get out!" cried Galen's dad. "There isn't much time."

Neshla couldn't move. "I can't breathe," she said.

"Galen, help me!"

Galen stood like a statue.

A sudden gush of water threw Galen off his feet.

He thudded against the wall. Galen shook his dripping head.

"What happened?" he asked.

"Get Neshla!" cried Dad.

Galen rushed to the airlock.
He grabbed Neshla and dragged her free.

The airlock door swished shut.

The creature beat its tentacles against the glass. The red eye bulged in fury.

"Three… two… one… activate," said Dad.

The airlock opened. The creature was sucked into space.

There was silence.

It was over.

"So much for a routine trip," said Neshla.

She looked at Galen. "Thanks," she said. "I knew my best friend wouldn't let me down."

"Come on," said Dad. "Let's have that dinner – vegetables only, of course!"

Everyone laughed.

The ship cruised silently through space.

It was time to go home.

Plant snacks

Carnivorous plants are plants that eat meat. They grow in poor soil that offers little nutrition. These plants have evolved over thousands of years and developed insect traps to snag, stick and capture their prey as a way of adding to their diet.

Meat-eating plants have names such as Venus fly trap, cobra lily, sundew, pitcher plant and butterwort.

North America has more flesh-eating plants than any other continent.

The bladderwort looks like a small, delicate plant, but is the fastest-known killer of the plant kingdom. It can capture a mosquito larva in a fraction of a second, using a clever trap door.

Once the victim has been sucked in, digestive juices pour over it. They are similar to those in the human stomach and slowly break down the insect flesh. Once the plant has eaten the soft tissues, anything left over is simply ejected.

Meat-eating plants fool their victims. The pitcher plant, for instance, has an upturned trap, which looks like a beautiful pitcher full of nectar. Curious insects land to take a sip but end up slipping to their deaths.

Once in, there is no way out.

A tiny insect might take several hours to digest. A fat fly, however, might take days.

Some pitcher plants are large enough to hold several litres of fluid. Even small rodents and birds have been known to come to a sticky end after stopping for a drink.

What sorts of plants are growing in your house?

Questions

Why is Galen's dad going to Vetron 5?

Who does Galen want to come too?

What does Neshla do when the ship lands?

What does Galen find in the pod?

What does the plant eat?

Where does Dad take the plant to?

What happens to make Galen wake up?

At the end, what does Dad want to cook?